SECOND GRADE, HERE I COME!

BY D. J. STEINBERG
ILLUSTRATED BY LAURA WOOD

GROSSET & DUNLAP

To the Incredible Mr. Dar—DJS

For Dad, my greatest teacher—LW

GROSSET & DUNLAP
An Imprint of Penguin Random House LLC, New York

Text copyright © 2017 by David Steinberg. Illustrations copyright © 2017 by Laura Wood. All rights reserved. First published in 2017 by Grosset & Dunlap, an imprint of Penguin Random House LLC, New York. Paperback reissued with stickers in 2020. GROSSET & DUNLAP is a registered trademark of Penguin Random House LLC. Printed in the U.S.A.

Library of Congress Control Number: 2017012019

Visit us online at www.penguinrandomhouse.com.

ISBN 9780515158083 (pbk)
ISBN 9780515158090 (hc)

18 17 16 15 14 13 12 11 10 9
10 9 8 7 6 5 4 3 2

BACK TO SCHOOL

No more lazy beach ball days.
No more summer getaways.
No more splashing in the pool.
No siree—it's back to school!
But there's one big ray of sun
even though vacation's done—
at least I know when summer ends,
it's time to see my old school friends!

THE GANG'S ALL BACK

Did Shayne get taller—or Zane get smaller?
Something's different there!
Camille got earrings,
Anne's all tan,
and Li got spiked-up hair.

Heath showed up with two big teeth,
and someone stretched out Zack.
We're all a summer older, but . . .
Hurray! The gang's all back!

FROM ME TO WE

Mr. Dar likes circles . . . *seriously!*
Today he drew one and labeled it *"ME."*
Then he circled that circle and wrote *"FAMILY,"*
and around that he drew a *"COMMUNITY."*

He made more circles—all itty bitty—
and circled them all to make up a *"CITY."*
He showed how more cities together create
a bigger circle that's called a *"STATE."*

Then states make "COUNTRIES," and on he went
to show how those make a "CONTINENT."
He drew one last circle, kind of like he began it,
and wrote the name "WE" on the big giant planet!

So that's how you get from "ME" to "WE"—
and how we are all stuck together, you see!

TEMPTATION

"If you might even be *possibly* tempted
to talk to a person near you,
go and change your place," says the teacher,
"right now before *I* do."

I look at my friend and my friend looks at me,
and soon as our guilty eyes meet,
I gather my things and head 'cross the room
to find a different seat!

SOCCER PRACTICE

My sweatpants have a hole in them,
and I'm not telling where,
but no matter what Coach Daniels says,
I'm not getting out of this chair!

SPELLING TEST

Every Friday morning,
we have our spelling T-E-X̶-S-T.
I'm not the greatest speller,
but I always do my B-E-X̶-S-T!

TAKE A LOOK AT MY BOOK!

Check out this book.
It's my new reading book,
and it's not like those little-kid books—
take a look!

It's chock-full of chapters and—
Hey! Wait a minute . . .
Excuse me, but why
are there *no pictures* in it?!

20 MINUTES A NIGHT

You have to read 20 minutes a night
when you are in grade 2.
It's only 20 minutes, I know,
but there's so much else to do!

I needed to play a game with my brother,

and talk to my friend about stuff,

and throw a ball so my dog won't get bored—
then my mom said, "Enough is enough."

So I opened the book—20 minutes was all—
and I figured I'd give it a try,
and I don't know how, but when I looked up,
a whole hour had whizzed right by!

"Just one more chapter!" I begged my mom.
"Enough is enough," she said.
Tomorrow I can't wait to read some more—
before it's time for bed!

TRYOUTS

I went to the school play tryouts,
but I tripped coming up the stage stairs.
Everyone giggled. I figured I'd blown it,
but then I decided, *who cares?*
I pretended to trip all over the place—
I stood up, then tumbled back down.
The kids laughed so hard, the teacher said,
"You're cast—in the part of the *clown!*"

HUNGRY ART

Art class comes before lunch,
so I'm in a hungry mood.
I guess that could be why
I'm always painting food!

RECYCLE WEEK

We're saving the planet this week—*hurrah!*
We're making no garbage at all,
except for the sort of recyclable kind
that can go in the box in the hall.

For lunch, we bring in reusable bags
with plastic compartments and seals,
then we pack them back up and . . . *YUCK*—what is *this*?
I forgot that bananas have peels!

My teacher says they're great for *compost*,
to help grow the garden at school.
Then he gives me two stickers, I hand him the peel—
let me tell you, recycling is *COOL*!

IT

Every day at recess,
you have to shout, "NOT IT!"
'cause if you didn't say it,
then you'll be "IT" legit!
But if you're "IT,"
don't pitch a fit—
just run around and flail,
and when you tag somebody else,
shout out, "YOU'RE IT!" and bail!

MARSHMALLOW TOES

On our way back to our classroom,
our teacher leads the two rows
and says not to make too much noise
by walking on *marshmallow toes*.

WALL OF DREAMS

The wall in the hall
says, "I have a dream . . ."
with a place for us kids to say
all the things we imagine
in our *own* dreams
how the world could be better someday.

The wall in the hall
is covered with dreams
for just about everything.
And although they're just dreams,
that's a good place to start,
like it was for the great Dr. King.

VALENTINE'S PARTY

I got three billion valentines,
but the one that is way off the chart
is the one that I got from my teacher—
it's a red-foil, milk-chocolate heart!

FRACTION ACTION!

I thought up a show called *Fraction Man*.
It made my friends all laugh.
When he's attacked by bad guys,
he divides himself in half.
Then he can keep on dividing himself
into clones that get smaller in size—
till the villain finds he's fighting off
sixty-four super-fierce little guys!

THE PRINCIPAL'S OFFICE

Someone passed a note to give the person next to me,
so I was just the delivery guy—*I'm innocent, you see!*
But when my teacher noticed, I was asked to leave the room
and sent to see the principal—
now I walk the hall of doom . . .

By the time I'm in her office, I've confessed my whole life of crime:
I was tardy for recess.
I drew in a book.
I swallowed gum one time!
The principal sends me back to class with a *smile*, for goodness' sake—
she says that even awesome kids are allowed to make mistakes.

NOODLE TIME

Our teacher's kind of funny.
Every day he plays a song
and makes us bop out of our chairs
to hop-skip-skoodle along.

The whole class wiggles and waggles
their arms and legs and kaboodles.
For exactly one minute, we dance and wave
like a bunch of second-grade noodles!

THE FUNNY THING ABOUT ZERO

Zero plus zero is zero.

I guess that could maybe be true . . .

But zero times a *thousand*—

how can *that* equal zero, too?!

DRIBBLE TROUBLE

We were practicing dribbling in gym today.
That ball had a mind of its own, I must say.
I was doing just fine
till I stopped at the line,
and that ball kept on

drib-

drib-

drib-

dribbling away!

MEASUREMENTS

When I went to the doctor, he measured me
and said I'm just *three foot eleven.*
That seemed kind of short, so I did some math—
in inches, that's *forty-seven!*
That sounded a little bit better—
still not great, if you know what I mean—
so I converted to centimeters,
where I'm a whopping *one hundred nineteen!*

END-OF-THE-YEAR BARBECUE

The Lesters invited us all to their pool—
the kids and the teachers, too—
to celebrate our class finishing school
with an end-of-the-year barbecue.

We played Marco Polo and tug-of-war,
wolfed down hot dogs with lemonade.
We took a few pictures and took a few more
and told stories about second grade.

When at last it came time to say our good-byes,
I felt one little tear,
and it gave me a shiver to realize
how much we've shared this past year.

And that's when it really struck me,
like that circle our teacher made,
this class has become *my* "COMMUNITY"—
and together we'll conquer third grade!

I had a dream for SUPERPOWERS

I have a dream that all cats are found. Especially Cleo